For Holly & Jodi, the original Gecko & Parakeet.
Which is which? We'll never tell . . .
—S.H. & L.P.

The illustrations for this book were created entirely in Procreate.

Cataloging-in-Publication Data has been applied for and may be obtained from the Library of Congress.

ISBN 978-1-4197-5091-5

Published in 2021 by Abrams Books for Young Readers, an imprint of ABRAMS.

Printed and bound in China
10 9 8 7 6

Abrams Books for Young Readers are available at special discounts when purchased
in quantity for premiums and promotions as well as fundraising or educational use.
Special editions can also be created to specification. For details, contact
specialsales@abramsbooks.com or the address below.

Abrams® is a registered trademark of Harry N. Abrams, Inc.

ABRAMS The Art of Books
195 Broadway, New York, NY 10007
abramsbooks.com

ITTY-BITTY KITTY-CORN

SHANNON HALE & LEUYEN PHAM

Abrams Books for Young Readers · New York

Kitty thinks she might be a unicorn.
A horn sits atop her fuzzy head, pointing
UP,
    UP,
        UP to the sky.
She feels so perfectly unicorn-y.

"Look at me!" says **Kitty**.

"You're not a unicorn,
putty-pie," says Parakeet.

"You're curled up like a cat,
fluffy-fry," says Gecko.

Kitty stands tall.

She prances on her pawed,
clawed, unicorn hooves.

She gallops on her
eensy-weensy unicorn legs.

"Look at me!" says
Kitty.

"You're still not a unicorn,
fuzzy-heinie," says Parakeet.

"You have a stubby tail,
teeny-tiny," says Gecko.

Kitty closes her eyes.

She concentrates.

And—Poof!—
her tail puffs up fat.

"Look at me!" says
Kitty.

"You're never going to be a unicorn,
funny-foo," says Parakeet.

"You meow in your sleep,
miffy-mew," says Gecko.

"Neigh," says **Kitty**.

"Neigh.
NEIGH."

She sticks her pink nose in their
ears in case they didn't hear.

"NEIGH!"

"You're a cat,"
says Parakeet.

"And that's that,"
says Gecko.

Still, **Kitty**'s unicorn
heart beats harder.

She lifts her front hoof and
sweeps her magnificent tail.

The sun is low; the shadows are long.
At last, she looks exactly how she feels.

"Ha-HA!
Look at me NOW!"
yells **Kitty**.

"Wow!" says Parakeet, astonished.
"Woo!" says Gecko, impressed.

Finally, they see me!

thinks **Kitty**.

Gecko points with his fat-tipped finger.
"Now, that's a **UNICORN**."

The **UNICORN** brandishes his **horn**.
He sweeps his magnificent **tail**.

He neighs a mighty

NEIGH.

Suddenly, **Kitty** feels
no bigger than a ball of lint.

flop

flop

flop

"Pardon me," says **Unicorn**.

"Yes?" squeaks **Kitty**.

"I so admire your fuzzy ears and silver whiskers,"
says **Unicorn**.

"You do?" says **Kitty**.

"And I wondered . . ."
UNICORN looks right
and then left.
"Did you know . . ."

"What?" says **Kitty**.

"Did you know . . ." says **UNICORN**, whispering now.

"What? WHAT?" yells **Kitty**.

"Did you know,"
says **UNICORN**,
"that I am a
KITTY-CORN?"

Kitty gasps.

Her tiny tail twitches with joy.

"Yes," says Kitty. "I see that now. You are a Kitty-corn. You are a fuzzy, furry, adorable Kitty-corn."

Unicorn nods. "I knew that another Kitty-corn like you would see."

"Yes," says **Kitty**.
"I see you."

Kitty and Unicorn are both Kitty-corns.

Kitty trots on her soft, teeny paws, and Unicorn pads on his huge, golden hooves.

They both like to toss their manes and brandish their horns.

They **both** like to scamper
after bumblebees . . .

and stretch out in a
patch of grass.

And when the sun is low . . .

their shadows merge till you can
no longer tell **one** from the **other**.